THE FISH PEOPLE'S CANYON

by Patrick H. Coleman

Patrick H. Coleman

PG – 17

p5906@webtv.net

ISBN-13: 978-1492260264

Book Design & Layout by redbat design | www.redbatdesign.com
Cover Photo © Fotosearch.com

Printed in the United States of America
First edition

I would like to dedicate this book to
the Rooster Rock State Park rangers and staff.

WOMEN OR GIRLS SHELL NOT
READ THIS BOOK !!!
Thank you !

CHAPTER 1

Half asleep, George reached for the bedside phone before it rang a second time. He glanced at the backlit alarm
clock next to the darkened lamp on the nightstand, but he
already knew it was another early start to his day. Inevitable phone calls before the break of dawn had motivated
his normally patient and understanding wife to set up her
own sleeping quarters in their guest bedroom several years
ago. Surprisingly, their marriage had actually improved.
George picked up the receiver, careful not to knock over
the glass of tap water next to the phone, and discreetly
cleared his throat before stating "Morning, Sheriff. Where
do you need me?"

As he drove Highway 14 toward Winter Park, George
took gentle sips from the perforated opening in the lid of

the container held in his right hand. The coffee smelled better than it tasted. It was piping hot and he appreciated the bitter sting in helping to sharpen his senses on another dark, chilly morning. Since late March, it was the third time this spring that a body had been found along the river. George hoped that this corpse would be different from the other two. The last thing needed in these parts was another serial killer. As the road meandered, he could make out a waning, crescent moon as it shone through the occasional breaks in the cloud cover. It seemed like a lonely god to George's sleepy mental state. He watched for it as it slowly drifted through the heavens, winking at him with a calm reassurance one moment, before coldly turning away and disappearing into indifference the next.

After turning off the highway onto a side lane, George wondered if and when he'd come across someone that he might recognize during one of these assignments. The last thing that a person wants to find at a crime scene is the familiar face of a neighbor, a friend, or a family member. As most must in his profession, he'd long ago learned to comfortably detach himself from the horror and avoid the gravity of grief that always accompanies the unexpected dead. He'd become fascinated with mortality and pathology as a boy before his formal studies as a young man. People often ask him how it is that he can stand such a morbid line of work. "Everybody dies and we all leave ourselves behind" is his usual reply. "Someone has to help figure it all out, clean up the mess, and put things to rest." If he hadn't found an undying love for the science behind his profession, he may have chosen a career cleaning up exhausted murder scenes, or a job that involved the rituals of burying the deceased.

Coming around a curve in the road, George could see the familiar flash and glow of the blue lights at the crime scene. They looked particularly eerie as they danced and played upon the reflective, rippled surface of the swiftly moving water. Along the bank of the river, the lights pushed and pulled the shadows up against the edges of the forest. The river rocks and fir tree branches seemed to pulse and shift as though they were impatient spectators changing seats to gain a better view of the show. The morning light had yet to break in the East, so the darkness that surrounded the impromptu riverside gathering seemed impenetrable and permanent. As he removed his evidence kit and satchel from the trunk, George zipped his coat up against the cold drizzle that steadily sprayed from the hazy reaches of the overcast sky.

Sheriff Parker's deputies were busy doing their unprepared best to survey and manage the area around the body. Crime tape was strung, distances were measured, and items were inventoried. "Thanks for getting over here so quickly, Doc," Larry Parker said as he held out his right hand for a cursory shake. With his left, the sheriff motioned for the spotlights to be turned on and aimed around the loosely strewn shape of the corpse. George set down his gear and got to work. Removing the same micro-cassette recorder that he's used since his University days, he began to quickly scan the body, reciting his observations as he worked through the preliminary steps of an examination that would continue in his lab back at the County Morgue. Taking a break from his monologue, he took out a camera and began to photograph the corpse from several positions and angles. The white flashes cut against the pulsing blue lights with a jumpy, strategic counter rhythm.

As George proceeded to note his observations, Larry spat from the wad of chaw resting in his lower lip and sat down upon his haunches across from the intently working coroner. Sheriff Parker patiently waited for a moment to insert his interruption. "Looks about like the others," Larry volunteered. George finished his own murmured thought and pushed the stop button on the recorder. "Yep," he finally answered. "Male, 25-30 years old, naked from the waist down. Drowning is the likely cause of death." George paused a moment. "But, I won't know for sure until the autopsy." Sheriff Parker stood up. "I can't tell you how many times," he explained, "that I've told these folks to be careful down by the river." George looked up from his work and asked, "Any idea who he is, Sheriff?" "Well," Larry answered, "I think he's the young man whose wife reported him missing a couple of nights back. She said he went out early in his boat, alone, to go fishing. Apparently, he never came back." George motioned for Larry to help roll the body for any additional evidence. "Boating accidents and unfortunate drownings aside," George began to share his curiosity through strained breath. "Isn't it bizarre that this is our third young man in as many months who turns up as a bare-assed corpse?"

"Yes, and no," Sheriff Parker answered as if navigating a balance beam. "Each of the bodies could have gotten tangled up in some underwater plants, tree branches, or other debris. Their clothes could have been torn off like that." "Sure," the coroner humored Larry, "but these young men could also be the victims of a killer." George continued, "If I'm not mistaken, then all three of the victims weren't just missing their pants, Larry. They were buck naked from the waist down." George stood up and began to pace around the corpse in a slow, methodical stroll. "Sheriff, it's almost as if these young men removed everything but their shirt and coat, entered the water, and later drowned."

Back at the morgue, Doctor George Madison worked through his normal routine of examining the body before an autopsy. After he looked over the lifeless form from head to toe, he addressed his attention upon the hands and fingernails. "Curious," he thought to himself. "This guy also has fish scales under his nails." Meticulously, he carefully scraped beneath each one and placed the tiny, slimy contents into a small jar. He would examine them later beneath a microscope in the adjacent lab. He took another sip from the black, bitter coffee that was always available in the small break room up the hall. It was warm, but not as hot as he liked it. Motioning for an assistant in another part of the morgue for help, the two men were soon hovering over the dead fisherman. They rolled the body over onto its side. George reached for his camera and began to photograph the deep scratches carved into the upper back and lower buttocks. The marks looked much like the wounds upon the previous bodies.

After relaying the body spine-down upon the examination table, the assistant couldn't help but remark that the victim's upper back looked like a more extreme version of his own after a wild night with a woman that he'd picked up from a local tavern a couple of years ago. "Not that I'm Casanova, or anyone like that," he commented, "but that lady couldn't help but carve up my backside as we wrestled out our drunken lust." The assistant smiled to himself. "Man, she was some wildcat" George raised his eyebrows and gave the younger man a knowing glance. "Fair enough, Romeo, let's check him for recent signs of sexual activity." After some work that left both men uncomfortably humble in their own masculine skin, George was able to confirm the assistant's conjecture. Sure enough, the exam showed that the fisherman ejaculated not long before his death. George quietly wished that he'd been shrewd to check the previous bodies for the same signs of pleasure before the men met their makers.

His brief regret was interrupted by the ringing of the telephone mounted next to the doorway. It was Sheriff Parker. As George listened, the Sheriff confirmed the identity of the dead man. He was, indeed, the husband who had been reported missing by his wife. One of the deputies found his boat anchored five miles upstream. "Okay, Larry," George said, "but tell me, my good man, were his clothes still on the boat?" "Yeah," Larry answered. "His wallet was still in the back pocket of his denims. Why do you ask?" Doctor Martin paused a brief moment before answering. "Well, it strikes as being mighty strange that each of the three drowning victims was discovered nearly naked." "Furthermore," George continued, "all three men had fish scales crammed beneath their finger nails."

"Sweet Jesus, Doc," the Sheriff protested in a highly pitched tone, "these men were out fishing, got careless, fell

into the river, and drowned. It is just a rash of similar accidents. Hell, maybe the moon was full and they each went
nutty for a spell." "You're probably right, Larry," George
humored his colleague, "but the coincidences are too unusual not to notice. Plus, the fish scales are really odd. At
a glance, they're not from any fish that I've ever caught
and eaten. They are definitely not salmon, sturgeon, or
trout." Catching his breath, George confessed, "I don't
know what species shed 'em."

"All right, Doc," the Sheriff's voice regained its com-
posure. "When you get a chance, send your samples over
to the University big wigs and we'll see what they can tell
us. I'll be at Joe's Diner around nine this morning. Stop
by if you have some time. I'll buy you a cup of coffee, you
can buy me a danish, and we can swap stories about the
one that got away."

CHAPTER 2

Early as usual, George sat at the table with the morning paper from the city under his arm. He ordered coffee from the waitress, placed the breakfast menu that she handed over next to the paper that was in front of him, and thanked her. It was as busy as ever for a Monday morning, but there always seemed to be room for more patrons. The smell of bacon and toast danced through the morning light amidst the speckles of dust and flashing shadows. He watched as the older couples slowly moved through their routines of eating, and sitting, and reading, and talking, and watching one another. He thought of the older Asian folks he'd seen in the park during fair weather mornings moving in a similar way, full of grace and patience. Waiting for his coffee, he began to leisurely skim over yesterday's news in between errant glances at advertisements, deals, and today's prices.

Sheriff Parker was always late. The problem wasn't that he was too busy, as George knew him to be, or overworked, as the Sheriff insisted on being. Larry Parker's 24-7 commitment stemmed from the fact that he was a bachelor who felt very obligated about his job. Instead, George figured that his problem with Larry's tardiness had everything to do with Larry's age. He was the youngest sheriff to hold the office as far as anyone can remember. Larry Parker was young and, as far as some folks were concerned, happened to harbor a bit of an attitude. That was all. It was simple enough. This attitude, however, just happened to include a separate set of rules for managing time and space such as always being late and feeling free to make phone calls at any hour of the day to whomever he liked.

Close to nine-thirty, Sheriff Parker pulled up, sauntered in, and sat down. George asked if he'd gotten any sleep. "Naw," Larry nodded to the side, "but sure wish that I had." The waitress came over and poured the sheriff a cup of very hot, very black coffee after giving the young man a wink and a brief greeting. The smell of the medium roast grind wafted over the table like a trucker's dream. "I was called out on a domestic violence case," Larry continued. "I just don't understand these goddamn women, Doc. This guy has beat her up three times and she still goes back to him. I told her if she doesn't leave him this time, she's only got herself to blame." George tapped his fingers on the table along either side of his empty cup. "You know what's going to happen to her? Someday, sadly, I'll likely meet her at the morgue and get paid to shake her hand." Larry clenched his chin to his lips and frowned. "Well, I hope that we're both wrong, Doc. It just makes me so goddamned angry. It's awful hard to help folks that refuse to help themselves."

The sheriff took a measured sip of his coffee, nodded a greeting to an older couple who were leaving a tip at a nearby table, and continued to share his sleepless, agitated thoughts. "They're so many damn things about this world that I just don't get." Larry sat up in his chair and reached for a toothpick from the dispenser on the table. "Last month, the District Attorney had us set up a special vice operation to catch johns down by the train station. All because a prostitute was found dead from a drug overdose." George Madison nodded. "Yeah, I remember her, that was some sad business." "So," the sheriff went on, "after a week, we caught three local men and two outsiders trying to pay for sex, arrested all of 'em, and put 'em through the system. Since the arrests, at least two of the local men have been not only fined and humiliated, but divorced by their wives. In my opinion, we did more harm than good."

George nodded again in agreement. "Sheriff, you are preaching to the choir. I still say we should legalize prostitution like they have in Europe and Australia. The people over there will tell you that a large city with districts allowing legalized prostitution makes for a much healthier society. Here in America, there are prostitutes everywhere. Rich men can pick up the phone and have one come to their hotel room any time of the day or night. It's the equivalent of ordering a pizza, but it's still illegal? You're right, Larry. It all seems stupid and ridiculous. We live in an upside-down world."

Sheriff Parker smiled at the waitress and thanked her after she refilled his cup. He poured a streak of sugar from the dispenser into the steaming brew and stirred it several times with the teaspoon that sat on the table next to the saucer. "Don't you also want the drug laws changed?" asked George, knowing the answer before Larry could start. The sheriff did not hesitate, "Yeah, I sure do. You know the way I look at it, Doc. Every American over the age of 21 has a constitutional right to be as stupid as they want as long as their stupidity doesn't interfere with my life. It would make my job a lot easier if I didn't have to mess with drug users and drug dealers. Legalize, or at least decriminalize, and it's a win-win situation for everybody."

George motioned to the waitress for some more coffee and then turned toward the sheriff. "I still don't fully agree with you, Larry." The sheriff raised a single brow. "I mean, look at all the problems that alcohol has given us." Sheriff Parker perked up at this, nodded, and said, "Yes, sure, but we could put a stop to most drunk drivers, if we could legally take their car away from them the first time that they're caught driving drunk. Then, we could sell the car and use the money to pay for drug and alcohol treatment programs. The addicts are sick, but the drunk drivers are irresponsible and dangerous. Just because they break the law, doesn't mean that they should be punished in the same way, or in the same place. We only have so many stones, Doc, and flocks of birds to kill."

George thanked the waitress for his full cup of coffee and gave an agreeing look to the possessed eye of the sheriff. "Look at the war on drugs with Mexico, Doc. It would be cheaper in the end to simply buy the drugs from the Mexican Cartels and destroy 'em." George nodded, smiled, and thought to himself that this man had a very good point. He imagined Larry down the road, no longer rethinking the law as a sheriff, but rewriting it as a congressman and a legislator. The role fit him well and being such a young sheriff, he could make it all happen with plenty of time for recreation and retirement.

"All right, Larry," George redirected the conversation. "Let's get back to what I was trying to tell you about the three young men who've managed to turn up dead from drowning in the last month." He sipped from his coffee and continued, "I checked with my coroner friend across the river in Oregon and he tells me they have five drowning incidents of their own with virtually the same circumstances. Normally, they have a fisherman reported drowned or missing every few years at the most. Say what you want, Sheriff, but there's something mighty strange going on out there on the Columbia River."

"Have you been talking to Crazy Old Man Jack?" Sheriff Parker couldn't help a snicker after he asked the question. "No," said George, "is he another drinking buddy of yours from high school?" "Naw," the sheriff replied, "he lives in a boathouse in the marina across from Hayton Island. He's a boozer who has some crazy stories to tell." Larry Parker stood up, put on his coat, and then picked up his hat and held it in his hands as he played with a frayed part of the brim. "I still say it's just a bad luck year for fishermen. I'll see you later, Doc. Tell Jack I said, 'Hello,' if you go and talk with him." With a smile tied around his head and the same saunter that he used to glide into the diner, the sheriff drifted out the same way, slow and quick all at once.

When George arrived back at his office, the lab report was atop his desk. He scanned it twice, then read it thoroughly after sitting down in his chair. He caught himself waving his hand in an absent-minded way as if there had been a buzzing insect hovering near his slightly sweaty brow. The words, "species not found," bothered him every time his eyes passed over the term. Either the findings will make for some happy biologists at the university, he thought to himself, or the sheriff's department is going to need a bigger net. "Both, probably" George mumbled. "I just hope they don't need a bigger boat, too."

CHAPTER 3

With the manic regularity of a rooster, the phone rang again at half past four in the morning. "Christ, Larry, what the hell have you got this time?" The sheriff let out a brief laugh and asked, "How do you always know it's me?" George rolled his tired eyes and slowly said, "Sheriff, you're the only person who calls me at this hour." The sheriff shifted his tone quickly when he added, "Always with bad news, too. We have another body. This time, I'm down at the park, just upstream from the I-5 bridge, not far from you in fact." George Madison sat up and slid his slippers on to his feet. "Don't tell me, Larry, this one's a young male and he's naked, right?" George frowned as Sheriff Parker said, "No, neither, Doc. I'll show you when you get here."

Twenty minutes later, George carefully looked at the fully clothed body. He finished the banana that he'd shown the good sense to grab on his way out of the house and tossed the peel away from the scene and into the dewy dark of the morning. Older than younger, the man was in his fifties and fully dressed. Wearing a utility belt, he was composed in the easy, practical manner of a construction worker. "I think he might've drowned, too," said George. "At a glance, I don't see any other apparent cause of death. We'll know more after the autopsy."

Back at the morgue, George stripped the body, looked it over from head to toe, and found nothing. An annoying and somewhat otherworldly flicker from a dying fluorescent tube peppered weak, sporadic light out from the corner of the lab. Occasionally, it would quickly darken and seem to patiently wait as the tired ballast gathered itself to push the power back where it was needed. George even liked the odd, resonant hum that played from the hanging fixture. It sounded like an alien ballad. Sometimes, he'd catch himself singing along in a mumble, or adding some odd, jury-rigged rhythm that suited his loosely musical sensibilities. Both he and the corner light were humming as he checked over the body one last time. There were no scratches along the back or buttocks as he'd found on the others. Checking again under the finger nails, however, George Madison was almost pleased to find what looked like more fish scales.

Leaving the muck-covered gloves on his hands, he immediately called Sheriff Parker. George was so excited about his discovery that he could hardly talk. "Larry, Larry," he stammered, "guess what? Fish scales... yes, Larry, fish scales under the body's finger nails. Now, what do you think of that?" The Sheriff was quiet for a moment, then he said, "Look, Doc, the salmon are running up the river by the tens of thousands. Everyone is out there fishing for them, bears included. This guy was probably fishing yesterday right along with the rest of the sportsmen." George was now yelling into the phone, "But, Larry, I told you, we haven't identified the fish. We may be dealing with more, here, than we realize." Sheriff Parker let out a confident sigh. "George, with all this global warming going on around us, maybe different types of fish are coming up the river. Maybe they moved up here from California. Hell, I don't know. Please, Doc, stop trying to make my job harder than it already is." With that, the sheriff hung up and left George to celebrate on his own.

"I can't let this go," George told himself. "There's something going on here that's not right." He put some of the fish scales into a small, sample bag to be sent down south to an independent lab that tests for DNA. As he was filling out the label for the package, the phone rang. It was the sheriff. "Hey, Doc, we just learned that our dead man was out working on the new dam being built up the Columbia at Rooster Rock. You wanna go for a drive? I need to talk with his foreman." "You bet," George replied with a smile. "It will give me a chance to clear my head."

* * *

The office for the new dam was located on the Oregon side of the river just off of I-84, just down stream from famous Rooster Rock in the Columbia River Gorge. Lewis and Clark rested there on their long, historical journey to the Pacific Ocean. This was where they first encountered the Native Americans of the Pacific Northwest. The Chinook lived in clustered villages near the water, allowing for easy access to the plentiful fish. They also gathered a variety of berries and dug up numerous edible roots that are common to the region. The quietly sophisticated culture was severely hampered by disease in the years that followed, but it has survived and continues to struggle in a land transformed and inhabited by outsiders. Outsiders who ultimately calmed the water of the Great Columbia, taming the churning, rushing river that had cut its way to the ocean for tens of thousands of years. Mother Nature was given a new habit and changed from vixen to nun. The tears of the Chinook were shed and mixed with the endless rains of the region. It is hoped that one day, these tears will lose their salt and return to change the Columbia back to its true, majestic form.

Further up the river is a big, beautiful cascade known as Multnomah Falls. Over 600 feet high, the steady wonder of water, light, and shadow has enchanted visitors and natives for hundreds of years. George proposed to his wife at the Falls and they return once a year to take a leisurely hike before enjoying lunch at the old lodge that overlooks the falling water. Driving past the falls, George thought of how much he loved his wife and how lucky he felt himself to be to have her in his life. He thought of calling her to remind her of this well-known fact as Sheriff Parker maneuvered the car up the gravel and past the gates into the administrative perimeter of the work site.

The two men walked up to the front of the office and Larry knocked on the door. A tall and very handsome young man opened the door with a smile and a phone to his ear. With his hand holding up an upright finger, the foreman mouthed the words, "I'll be right with you," and quickly began to finish the interrupted conversation. "Mr. Larson," Larry stated after the phone was hung up, "we are here to ask you if you know this man and when you last saw him." He showed him a photo of the dead man taken the previous year under better circumstances. Jake Larson took one look and answered, "Yeah, that's Bob Daniels. He has been working down here for a couple of months now. Is he in trouble?" With a measured frown and a well-practiced tone, Sheriff Parker delivered the bad news. "We regret to inform you that his body washed up on the Washington side of the river near Vancouver this morning. We're wondering if you can tell us how he got into the river."

The foreman furrowed his brow, raising his eyes as he slowly shook his head and sat down behind his desk. "I haven't the faintest," he volunteered. Looking across the room at a list on a clipboard hanging near the door, he said, "Bob was scheduled to work last night. When he didn't show, we called him, but got no answer." The Sheriff nodded and asked, "Was he working down by the water?" "Yeah," the foreman responded, "but we tell everybody to wear a safety harness. He should have been fine." Sheriff Parker walked over to the clipboard and began to examine the names, dates, and assignments. "Without the harness, is it possible that he could have slipped, had a fall into the river, and drowned," asked the Sheriff, "without anyone noticing?" "Well, it was storming fierce that night, so yeah, maybe." The foreman grabbed his empty mug from the desktop and walked over to the coffee maker near the opposite wall. "You guys want a cup? Help yourself if you do." George eyed the stained, half-filled pot of oxidized coffee with suspicion.

"He was working alone down there," the foreman continued, "because the other guy has been out sick with the stomach flu. Bob's experienced and kind of a loner any-

way, so we let him pull a couple of shifts on his own, doing what he could. We've got deadlines pressing as you can
guess. The vandalism hasn't helped any." "Vandalism?"
Sheriff Parker asked as he finally took a seat across from
the foreman's desk. "Yeah, you might remember hearing
about the protests up this way before the project pushed
through. They were active in Salem, too. A lot of folks
were none-too-happy when they learned about the plans
to build a dam here. After we started construction, the
protests stopped, but now it seems like we're having problems with vandalism and trespassing almost every night.
The State Sheriff's Department has all the reports."

As Sheriff Parker stood up to shake hands with the
foreman, George quietly looked over the different clip-
boards that hung in slightly uneven rows on the wall near
the door. He wrote down Jake Larson's name and phone
number on the back of a car wash voucher that had ex-
pired, neglected, still resting in his wallet. "C'm on, Doc,"
Sheriff Parker said as he patted George on the back. "Let's
get out of this man's hair." Jake Larson stood up to see
them to the door and retrieve his hard hat and jacket that
hung in the corner. He placed the hat over his head and

walked to his truck, nodding to the men as he listened to the crunch of wet gravel beneath the tires of the car as it slowly drove toward the gate.

CHAPTER 4

George Madison decided to wait until he was back at his office to telephone the foreman. He persuaded Jake to meet him for lunch the next day, as the foreman had Sunday off from work. They met at what George described as a "great little Shari's" just off the highway in Troutdale. The foreman knew the place and was standing next to his truck when George pulled up across the restaurant parking lot. There was a respite from the morning rain and George enjoyed sucking in the crisp, breeze-blown air. As he walked toward the foreman. George was teased by a memory from his youth and with a subtle sense of play, he avoided the reflections of the clouds hiding in the puddles and standing water that mottled the pavement. "Morning," George greeted Jake and the men shook hands, entered the restaurant, and were seated.

"I have to warn you," the foreman confessed. "I'm not a cheap date." George smiled and told Jake to order anything that suited him, including onions. The men both shared a laugh as the waitress poured their coffee. George didn't want to come across as a kook, but he felt that he needed to share everything that had happened. Watching the older couples and well-dressed families enjoying their brunch after church, George asked the foreman if Bob Daniels was a fisherman. "Strangely enough, he wasn't," Jake answered. "He was from Nevada and loved to take out his dirt bike and tear-ass around the hills. Fishing was too slow for him. He had no patience for it."

Buttering his Belgian waffle, George asked the foreman if he knew how Bob could have gotten fish scales wedged under his finger nails. "Fish scales? Maybe he grilled some trout for dinner. We didn't have any mutual friends outside of the job. Like I told you before, he was kind of a loner. Don't you guys cut into their stomachs after death to look for poison and booze and stuff?" "Sure," George replied. "He had what looked to be a hamburger in his system, along with fries and a milkshake. There wasn't any fish." Jake shrugged his shoulders and cut into the slice of ham that sat before him in the orange yoke of an over-easy egg.

After a sip of water to wash down a bite of food, George said, "I don`t have all the facts yet, but I think that your worker was murdered." "What?" Jake said in an uncomfortably loud voice. Catching himself and bringing his volume down, he asked, "What makes you think that? You said he drowned." George agreed with an easy nod. "He did drown, along with three other young men found washed up on the Washington side of the Columbia. Those four and five others found on the Oregon banks have been found dead in the last two months. Apart from Bob Daniels, the other men were reportedly out fishing on the river." George took another sip of water. "Here's where it gets kind of nutty. In each case, the deceased was found to have fish scales under one or more of his fingernails. Moreover, the scales are unlike anything on record. We might have a new kind of fish on our hands."

The foreman asked if the scales didn't come from "one of them invasive species from Asia." Jake contin-ued, "There are some real-to-life monsters swimming in the waters of the world, and I'm not talking about sharks and crocodiles. There are some scary fish out there and a bunch of them have been brought into our own backyard. Nothing preys on them and they lay eggs like crazy. I seen 'em on television: wild, alien-looking things with teeth as long as your pecker." George laughed. "Anyway, I'm no Jock Coostow, or anyone, so how do you want my help with this?" Jake asked. "You're talking to a hunter who likes watching sportsman shows on the tube."

George smiled and thanked Jake again for his time. "I guess that I'm looking for some moral support from someone other than my wife," he confessed. "The Sheriff is convinced that it's just a lousy streak of carelessness and bad boating. I asked you to see me, because I'd like to know more about the vandalism at the dam site." The foreman nodded and wiped some yoke from his chin with his well-soiled napkin. "Well," he started, "it always happens during the night, as you might expect, but we never see anyone, or any signs of trespassing, like broken locks, cut fence, or unusual tire tracks. The Sheriff's Department has been over everything, twice. The vandals must be coming along the river by boat." Finishing his second cup of coffee, Jake continued, "The Columbia is really swift along the work site. The bastards would need a motor to get to us from the water, but the night crews never hear a sound outside of their own work. For a stretch, we contracted a local security firm and they assigned two guards down by the river for a three-week stretch. They didn't see, or hear, a damned thing and every morning we'd find something messed up."

"Like what?" asked George. "Well, they tore down scaffolding several times, and have repeatedly damaged a bunch of concrete forms. The vandalism always occurs near the water. I keep waiting for them to slash tires, or break into our facilities, but that hasn't happened, yet. It all needs to stop. Insurance covers a lot of the damage, but we're falling behind schedule in a bad way." George frowned and asked, "Could they be using scuba gear?" Jake shook his head. "They'd have to be the best swimmers in the world to get through that current. Either that, or they are part salmon."

George finished the last bite of his second breakfast that morning. "Jake, would you be willing to take a drive with me and track down a man who might be able to shed some light on what's going on out there on the water?" The foreman looked at his wristwatch, thought to himself for a brief moment, and said, "Sure, who is he?" George motioned to the waitress for the check before answering. "Sheriff Wilson told me about him. Apparently, he's lived on the river in an old house boat for the better part of forever. The way Larry described him, he might be half-salmon, himself."

CHAPTER 5

The marina where old man Jack lived wasn't far from the restaurant, so Jake followed George in his truck. On the way, George pulled into a state-run liquor store and picked up a bottle of bourbon. The Sheriff mentioned that the old guy was a drinker, as well as a recluse, so George figured that a very belated houseboat warming gift was a good idea. Parking on a bare patch of shoulder, the men walked down the long ramp to the boat house. As they approached the docks, they heard a radio and saw a man working on his houseboat, dancing a bit as he varnished. After a proper Sunday greeting, George asked, "Do you know a character by the name of Jack? He's supposed to live down here on the water." The man set down his brush and responded, "Do you mean Crazy Old Man Jack?" "Yeah," said George, "he sounds like our man." Picking his brush back up, he used it to point down the pier. "He's in the last boat down on the right. If you end up in the river, then you went too far." The man took up some more varnish from the can at his feet and warned, "You best be careful when you approach him, though. He can be an ornery old cougar when he's at the bottle." George held up the sack in his left hand and said, "We've come prepared. Thanks for the warning."

As they approached the old man's boat, the men were far from surprised by its condition. They could smell it before they saw it. The boat listed to the right and seemed almost hungover, or sick. It was a sad excuse for a dwelling and looked more like a hole that someone digs for himself to hide inside and wait for death. A hole that floats. George knocked on the weatherbeaten door, loosening a few flakes of faded green paint that fell to his feet and mixed with the unswept detritus that looked to be an inch thick in the best of places. George wondered if the man had ever cleaned the top side of his boat. After several more attempts to rouse a response, they saw a soiled curtain move in one of the little windows near the entrance. They heard muffled cursing and some shuffling about

---

from within the cabin during a long, tired moment before the door finally creaked open. The smell of cat urine, stale tobacco smoke, and rotten fish was almost overwhelming. Emerging slowly from the darkness and the stench was a man that looked older than the Moon.

"What do you guys want, now?" the old man challenged his unwanted guests. "I'll send another check at the end of the month." George smiled, raised his eyebrows, and held out his right hand for a shake. "My name's George Madison, Clark Country Coroner, and this is Jake Larson. He's a foreman working at the new dam site up the river. We didn't come for your money, old timer." George continued, taking the bottle out of the sack and handing it to the old man, "Sheriff Wilson told me that you have a strange story to share and we came hoping to hear it." The old man's demeanor changed, instantly. With a smile and newfound spirit, he eyed the label, eagerly licked part of his upper lip, and said, "Well, it's about time someone came to talk to me. I've waited some forty-odd years to tell my tale." The old man unscrewed the cap, took a long swig from the bottle, and exhaled as he motioned his guests toward some dilapidated deck chairs. "You'd think that I was seeing fairies, or getting myself abducted by them little aliens in those flying saucers. Hell, I'm old, and I'm a drunk, but I'm not crazy."

After some effort to clear a variety of seemingly random objects from the seats, including three decoy ducks, a life preserver, two boxes of newspapers, and a stuffed iguana, the three men sat down. The old man offered a taste from the bottle, but his guests politely declined each time it was raised. "I'm warning you guys," the old man began, "bottle, or no bottle, if you came here for a laugh at my expense, I'll toss you back where you came." The old man grimaced with an angry pride. "Don't think that I can't, either, just because I'm long in the tooth." His demeanor inspired a reassuring chuckle from his guests. "Jack, I assure you," George volunteered, "that our business is nothing short of serious." The coroner straightened his smile, leaned forward and said, "Over the past two months, eight young men have been found dead and drowned on both sides of the Columbia." The old man exclaimed, "I knew it!" and slapped his thigh. "I knew it when I read about a couple of them fellers that got washed up." Validated, Old Man Jack pulled again from the now half-empty fifth of bourbon. Satisfied, he turned and looked out over the water in an angry squint and declared, "It's them damned She-Devils!"

As the old man stood, lost in the past, George noticed that his body was oddly bent to the left. Watching Jack sit back down, the coroner smiled to himself as he realized that the old man's curious posture must have come from living on a listing boat for so long. Either that, or he was born that way and found a home to suit the odd angle of his stance. "Forty years ago," the old man began his old man's story, "when I bought this here boat, I also bought some security." Disappearing into the cabin for a moment, Jack emerged with a rather large spear gun. "I wanted to be down here by the water, so if I see that she-devil again, I can finally kill her." As the old man took another drink from the comfort of his bottle, George asked, "What in the world is a 'she-devil' and why do you want to kill it so badly?"

"Well," the old man settled down, "when I was young, that devil bitch stole away with my manhood." George sat back in his chair and crossed one leg over the other. "How did she do that?" The old man told his audience how, back in his early twenties, he was up early one morning during salmon season. "I took my boat out on the river in almost perfect calm. The water was like glass and there was a fog upon it as thick as my mother's pea soup. There was a big run of Coho salmon that year and my plan was to catch at least three during the outing. I anchored my boat about a hundred yards from shore and right away I caught a big one. I was unhooking it when I heard a big splash off to starboard. When I looked, there was nothing but water and fog. I went to drop my freshly baited line and I noticed some movement out in the water." The old man gently shook his head from side to side. "She was the most beautiful woman I ever saw, just swimming toward my boat like it was a pleasant summer afternoon."

"I could only see her head at first, so I yelled out to her and asked if she was okay. She stopped swimming about fifty feet from my boat and just stared at me as she treaded at the water. When I shone my light on her, I could see she was even more beautiful than I thought, but there was something funny about her. Her skin had a light, greenish glow to it and her lips were softly painted pink, like a beautifully cooked salmon. The woman had long, light blue hair and beneath it, her eyes reflected my light in a haze of cobalt. She was like a young fisherman's dream come true." The old man lingered on this image in his mind and pulled from the bottle. After a moment, he stood up and continued his story. "I lowered my voice and greeted the woman, again, offering my open hand to her. It was all I could do not to jump in and swim toward her. I felt like I was coming under a spell."

The old man supported his weight on the back of the chair and stared past the men toward some undefined point in the distance hidden within the light of the sunlight penetrating the clouds and the dappled glare from the water. The wind was up and whitecaps were sprouting and blooming across the face of the river. They could hear an eagle nearby, calling to its mate, and a group of gulls flitted about the pier and chatted among themselves, contemplating a flight further inland. "When she spoke," the old man picked up his tale, "it was like she used a perfect voice that I'd only ever heard in my head. Just the sound of it rippled through my body and gave me the shivers. I can still feel them shakes. She asked if I liked her and I could barely respond, dumbstruck by her beauty and the angelic sound of her voice."

"'Who are you?' I wondered aloud, but she didn't say. Instead, she wanted my help. 'Of course,' I told her, 'swim over and I'll help you out of there.' Then, she rose up out of the water, erect-like, as though she was just a standing there before me." The old man took a swig from the bottle and wiped his mouth on the sleeve of his windbreaker. "I could spy her breasts and they were the prettiest that I ever did see. There were like honeydews, perfectly shaped, glistening and glowing like the northern lights. Her nipples were dark green and slightly upturned, like flowers stretching toward an inevitable sun, impatiently waiting for the light to break through the morning fog." George wasn't sure if the fountain of poetry had been hiding in the old man, or freed from the bourbon bottle. The coroner was daydreaming of champagne genies when he heard something strange that brought him back to his seat.

It sounded like a murmur, or a muttering, at first, but after a moment, it was obvious that Crazy Old Man Jack had started to sing to himself. It didn't take George long to recognize the Hallelujah Chorus. The sound was soft, but it quickly built in volume as the old man let himself go and seemed to dance with inspiration on a Sunday's afternoon. It seemed to George that the bourbon was starting to kick in and the coroner looked over at Jake. The two men shared a smile as they listened to Jack's off-key rendition of Handel. Interrupting himself suddenly, the old man returned from the heavens and declared, "Man, when I saw those boobies, I swear to Christ that I could plainly hear the Mormon Tabernacle Choir singing like angels on a mission."

Impatient, the foreman began tapping at the face of his wristwatch. George nodded reassuringly to Jake, and then gave his attention back to the old man. "Go on, Jack, what happened next?" The old man put the bottle down near the duct-taped leg of his chair and displayed a crooked finger from his outstretched arm. "She pointed toward the shore and said, 'Will you come with me?' Her voice echoed in my head. I was so taken by it... and her, that I stripped off my clothes and jumped in the water. I don't know how I didn't freeze to death. Blue-balled, the only thing that I was wearing was a sportsman fixed blade in a sheath strapped below my left knee. I must have been so hot and bothered that I plum forgot to take it off along with everything else." The old man adjusted his crotch with his free hand and kicked at an empty cat food can near his feet. "So," he went on, "I followed the woman to where the water shallowed, but she stayed just ahead of me, luring me with that voice and the blue glint of her eyes. Near the bank of the river, she turned and rose from the gently lapping surface of the river. Again, she revealed her beautiful chest and lithe little tummy. I pushed my way through the water and reached my hands out to her as I drew closer."

"As she shut her eyes, mine shut too, and I started to feel like I was floating. Then, she started singing the sweetest lullaby that I ever did hear." The old man picked up the bottle and began to unscrew the top. "It was like I'd heard it before, you know, from my mother, or grand-mother, and yet I still can't place the damned tune." The old man drank from the bottle and closed his eyes with the hope of more clearly resurrecting his memory of that morning. "Before I knew what was happening, she was holding me in her arms, just a stroking me and caressing me as softly as she sang that tune. I felt so peaceful like, and roused, like a teenage boy waking up on a Friday morning. It felt like she was sending electricity all through my body. I was so warm, even though the water was chilly. Every part of my body wanted this woman right there and then. I reckon that's why I didn't take notice of the webbing between her fingers until it was too late. The beautiful bitch was part fish!"

George coughed, "Do you mean she was a mermaid?" The foreman chuckled to himself and interrupted, "I wanted to catch me one of them, but I never had space for a big-enough aquarium." The old man opened his eyes, scowled a bit, and peered over at Jake with a steely look. "You don't catch mermaids, they catch you." The old man sneered, before relaxing his face. "Anyhow, I don't like to use that word. People just laugh when they hear 'mermaid,' like your friend here," and Old Man Jack looked at George with his thumb tossed toward the foreman. "They dismiss the whole thing as some kind of fantasy." The old man pulled at the bottle, slowly working his way through its copper comfort. "Hell, I know it sounds fantastic and all, but it were no fantasy. That damned she-devil seduced me. Hell, you might even call it rape. She started with lul-labies and being gentle and sexy and all, but once she had me where she wanted me, the bitch took advantage." The old man pulled into himself, either embracing his shame, or avoiding it with the bourbon as he took another sip. "She was so strong," he continued, "and I felt so weak, like when you're in a nightmare, but you can't move fast enough to run away from what's after you."

The old man sat forward with his head lowered. "She held me and kept me inside her even after I finished," he went on, his knees knocking together. "I squirmed a bit, but I couldn't get free. I can't tell you how long it was that she sang to me, just holding my spent body flush against her own with the water lapping against us. I recovered my strength some, but couldn't tell you how long it took. I must have been half-asleep. With a whisper, she finished her strange song and held me even tighter. Then, she be-gan swimming with me in the direction of my boat." The old man offered the bottle up to his guests one last time, before he drank himself after their polite decline. "I fig-ured that she was just taking me back, safe and sound, like after the prom."

The old man drank, tipping the bottle up, and finished the fifth of bourbon. "Boy, was I wrong. The bitch started holding me tighter and then pulled me down into the calm water. It was everything I could do just to draw in a decent breath. I tried to push her away from me, but her grip was too strong. As I wrestled with the she-devil, my left hand brushed against the sheath of my knife. I drew it, slashing and stabbing at the thing until she brought us back to the surface. I cut her neck pretty good and that must have done it. Still in her clutches, I gasped at the cool air above the water and caught my breath. I still can't believe what I saw next." The old man slowly shook his head from side to side, stared at the floor with distant, booze-glazed eyes, and said, "The eight-inch gash in her neck closed itself up and seemed to heal as I watched. I cut her again above her beautiful breast and she screamed a terrible, unearthly wail, but the ugly wound seemed to close as fast as my fixed blade had opened it. The monster ripped and tore at my back with her hands and the pain of her nails was sharp enough to keep me focused." The old man's breathing quickened as he relived the experience. "I brought the knife behind her and stabbed, again and again, but she just held me tighter. Her anger peaked and she howled like a banshee, slowly squeezing the life out of me like a mouse in the embrace of a boa constrictor." The old man held himself and rocked back and forth in his chair. "Drawing quick breaths," he continued, "I fought the urge to panic, losing my strength in the fight. Then she just smiled and dragged me back down into the blackness of the water."

The coroner looked over at the foreman and the two men quietly wondered if they were listening to a ghost sharing a nightmare dredged from the Unknown. The old man became still and slowed his breathing. He looked at the rapt faces of the small audience in front of him and frowned before saying, "I didn't know what to do next, so I guess my instinct took over. I brought the knife to the top of my willy and used the serrated edge to saw and cut and hack it off. The she-bitch looked at me in shock through the murkiness of the water and we shot to the surface of the river. I gasped and stabbed at her as I fought to focus my thoughts away from the pain. Finally, she let go after I plunged the blade into her left eye. Bleeding badly, I dog-paddled back to my boat in a shiver as I listened to the hellish sound of her fury. To this day, I'm still not sure how I made it. I managed to stuff some towels into the wound and slow the loss of blood before I passed out. I woke up on a vet's table. I guess a couple of fisherman heard the racket of those ungodly screams. Anyway, they motored over to the scene and found me half-dead, then took me to the nearest hospital—a veterinary hospital." The drunk old man surprised his guests with a warm smile. "I reckon that animal doctor turned me into the old sea dog you see today."

The old man pressed his hands down upon the arms of the chair and pushed himself up, knocking over the empty bourbon bottle. It rolled away on the deck of the houseboat with a sound that signaled the end of the story. Finding his balance, he turned his back to his guests and lifted his shirt to reveal an ugly display of scars that crisscrossed and swirled, forming a kind of treasure map whose only riches were bad memories. Then, he slipped off an old, worn belt and dropped his faded trousers to the floor, turning toward the men to reveal what was left of his sex after the self-administered molestation. Neither George, nor Jake, had much stomach to bare the sight before their eyes, so each man turned away after confirming the shock and painful awe of the old man's yarn.

Pulling up and fastening his pants, Old Man Jack stepped inside the cabin of his boat, reemerging a moment later with a small baby food jar. He handed it to George, saying, "I pulled these out of the wounds in my back." George held the jar up to get a better look and counted several shards of what looked like green-tinted fingernails. "Jack, may I take these back to my lab for analysis? I'll return them when I'm done." The old man smiled. "Sure, just make sure that there's another bottle, or two, for the privilege. Them's genuine fish-girl nails. I bet they're worth a fortune."

CHAPTER 6

The following week found George feeling like a kid waiting for Christmas. After sending out a sample of the old man's catch for proper analysis, George spent much of the week getting ahead of a light workload, but his mind was littered with thoughts of glistening scales, greenish fingernails, and mysterious fish women. He thought of the drowned men, too, and of the chronic vandalism at the dam construction site. In his gut, he knew that the nails were related to the scales and would come back as a DNA match, but he needed formal confirmation before he updated Sheriff Wilson. He was convinced that everything was connected. The coroner only had a theory, but he thought it was sound in attempting to piece together the puzzle. Folks would likely laugh at the idea of mermaids existing, but dismissing evidence like DNA is the equivalent of rejecting the truth. Thursday afternoon, George got what he wanted and his genuine mystery was confirmed. He glanced over the rest of the analysis, but his excitement kept bringing his eyes back to briefly stare into a long, two-dimensional box two-thirds down the second page of the report. In black type, unadorned by ribbons or bows, sat the words, 'Species: Unknown.'

The next morning, George ran into the sheriff outside of the downtown coffee shop. Larry couldn't help but notice the stack of books and folders that George held like a school-age kid. The coroner took up the sheriff's offer of a sandwich and a coke, taking the opportunity to bring Larry up to speed. More than once, the sheriff could be easily heard laughing out loud as George relayed the adventures of Old Man Jack, along with his own ideas about what it was that was taking the lives of young men along the water. Finishing his chicken-fried steak, the sheriff told George to "Go talk to Chief Thunder Cloud. He's the head of the Chinook tribe just up river. I have his number back at the office. Stop by, later, and pick it up." The sheriff gave the coroner a wry smile. "That old indian might know something about Old Man

Jack's mermaid. He has enough stories to keep you listening all day long."

After lunch, George poked through the book stacks at the nearest state college. He always loved the smell of libraries and made the most of his afternoon searching through its treasure. Moreover, he loved the common quiet. He wondered to himself if his enjoyment of silence lead to a career working with the dead. That afternoon, with a banker's box worth of research material against his belly, he picked up the phone number from the sheriff's office and drove home. He devoted his weekend to reading what looked to his wife to be countless articles, essays, and documented reports of mermaids and mermaid sightings. That evening, she brought a plate of dinner into his den with a third request to take out the trash from the kitchen. Without looking up from the open book on his desk, George politely asked his wife not to nag him. "That's part-woman, part-horse," she told him. "Are nags related to mermaids?" Smiling, George answered, "No, not unless they're centaurs." They shared a laugh, then he stood up and gave her a big hug followed by a little kiss. The trash would have to wait until later.

That night, George dreamt that he was an old retired sailor, living in a lighthouse with his wife. They couldn't get the lamp to work and a fog was moving toward the shore. The dense, grey mass pushed forward over the water, enshrouding a rapidly setting sun. Working feverishly, they heard a voice call up to them from below like a wave crashing upon the rocks. Leaving his wife standing next to her myriad reflections in the mirrors of the unlit lamp, he rushed down the spiral staircase. The strange voice grew louder and more resonant. He quickened his pace and seemed to dance down the steps, but the stairs wouldn't end. The darkness grew cold around him. He stopped and shivered, feeling his bones chill as the fog crept toward him up the stairwell. The unearthly voice seemed to blow upon his ear in a heavy whisper, then he heard his wife calling down to him from the gallery, "Wake up, sweetheart. George, you're dreaming, wake up." Disoriented, he laid in bed for an hour afterward and stared at shadows on the ceiling, listening to the murmur of the radio before falling back asleep.

* * *

Up early, the coroner brewed a pot of coffee, relieved the kitchen of its garbage, and went to work in his study. During his library research the previous day, George photocopied numerous magazine articles, photos, and drawings from the periodical collections and newspaper files. As the dawn light crept into the house and reached around the curtained windows, he carefully organized the material into a binder, meticulously reading and examining each entry. Later that morning, with the makeshift scrapbook open beneath his nose, he shuffled about the house every hour looking for his wife with whom to share a picture, or read aloud a particular entry. It was a work in progress that made him feel equal parts pride, excitement, and youth.

Standing outside of the closed bathroom, George threaded his voice through the frame and the door toward the uninterested ears of his better half. "Did you know that sightings of mermaids are still reported all around the world?" The muffled, but well-measured voice of his wife returned to him from the inside of the bathroom, "No, dear. I didn't know that." George couldn't help himself and launched into an impromptu history lesson. "Yeah, and they go way back, at least to the Chinese and the ancient Greeks. Sailors have been seeing mermaids as far back as anyone can remember. Plus, the stories they still tell of their encounters are very similar, if not identical, but the tales are usually separated by hundreds of years and thousands of miles of ocean." The door opened and his wife, conservatively dressed for a brunchy bridge party with her lady friends, said, "That's nice, dear," and gently pushed past his wide eyed enthusiasm into their bedroom just down the hall.

She was reaching up into the closet for a different purse as George stood behind her. Oblivious of her efforts, he read, "They lured men into the water with their beauty and then drowned them." He closed the binder and set it on the bed as his wife smirked and pointed at the purse that she wanted for her outfit. George reached up and lifted it down to her, saying, "That's totally classic mermaid legend, if you ask me. There's another story from the fifteenth century about a fishing boat that accidentally netted a mermaid in the Mediterranean. The crew tied her up and tried to keep her, but the creature's beauty bred jealousy and madness in the men. To save his ship, the captain threw her overboard." Purse in hand, his wife smiled back at him and suggested, "Don't share that with your old Navy friends, particularly the married officers. You'll likely give them bad ideas."

That afternoon, George spent some time on the telephone. First, he made a number of calls until he reached the spokesperson for the chief of the Chinook tribe that live near Celilo Falls. George was told that Chief Thunder Cloud would "meet with the doctor" on Sunday, around two, or as the voice put it: "When the bear stops fishing in the river." Making himself a cup of tea, George telephoned the foreman, next. "Are you up for another adventure?" he asked Jake. "Sure," the foreman answered, "as long as you're doing the driving. Plus," he added, "it'll cost you another lunch." George hung up the phone after thanking Jake for his help and stepped out for the mail and the afternoon paper. Settling into his chair a half-hour later, he enjoyed a leisurely nap before his wife returned from her luncheon.

* * *

Late Sunday morning found the two men traveling east through a steady downpour of chilly rain. The interior of the car was warm and smelled of light-roast coffee and aftershave lotion. The chatter of the news mixed with the squeak of the wiper blades against the glass. It performed a curious concert over the steady din of the engine and the ventilated air blowing against the defogged windshield. They were headed into a part of the Columbia River Gorge that Jake had never seen before. He couldn't help but comment on how beautiful it was, anymore than he could restrain his sense of humor. "This is some *Gorge*-ous country, all right." The coroner winced, then followed his playful grimace with a chuckle. "Are you sure that it isn't *George*-ous?" he mused and the men laughed together.

The foreman continued, "I get out and about plenty since I moved up here from southern California, but I tend to go to Portland, or head toward the coast. I never seem to get out this way, unless it's for work." George reached his hand beneath the dashboard and turned down the radio. He loved any and all opportunities to share his love for the country that he's called home for much of his life. "The Columbia River Gorge began forming some twelve million years ago, if you believe that the planet is older than the Bible tells us. The river begins up in Canada and runs down, forming a neat, but unnecessary, border between the great states of Washington and Oregon on its journey to the Pacific. It has supported human habitation for some thirteen thousand years." Jake laughed to himself, "Then it's almost as ancient as Crazy Old Man Jack."

They passed Rooster Rock State Park and Multnomah Falls as George held the wheel with both hands, guiding the nose of his car through the sporadic gusts of wind. Jake looked up at the cascading spray along the cliff face and watched the water mingle with the rain. George interrupted the moment by saying, "You know that your dam is going to drown this area and change it for the worse. That's why so many people are upset. It isn't just the environmentalists that are pissed, either. Changing the river will change the entire way of life for people that have called this place home a hell of a lot longer than you or me." Jake nodded, reluctantly, before countering with "Sure, but folks will raise a bigger stink when they don't have enough electricity to power their homes and businesses. Besides, the more this country changes, the more it stays the same. They'll land on their feet." George nodded in agreement, but he wasn't sure that the Chinook wouldn't land somewhere else, displaced like so many other natives of North America, forced to swim in bottles of whiskey instead of the river as they nursed the pain of losing their land, along with their livelihood upon it.

The Storm let up as they arrived at the village near Celilo Falls. Neither of the men had seen anything quite like it. They drove past a great building called a Longhouse. Gawking at the site like he was at an outdoor museum, George brought the slowly moving car to a stop several yards short of a boy who was playing in the road. No more than six, he waved a stick around and occasionally swiped at a loose pile of three small stones. The boy looked up at the men, stepped to the side of the car, and stared at them through the rain-spattered windows and slashing wipers as though they were ghosts. George felt a gentle chill run up his spine. Driving on, Jake said to George, "We're not in Kansas, anymore," and the men looked and pointed at the different houses painted a variety of once bright, but now weatherworn colors. George said, "When I telephoned, I was told me that the chief lived in the box that looked like the sky on a high summer's day. I'm thinking that's it," and he threw a chin in the direction of a modest, but very blue house. George pulled the car over to the side, let the engine idle a moment, and then turned off the motor, waiting for it to choke out the effort of getting them there. Happy to be standing, Jake stretched his arms into the gently misting rain as George grabbed his jacket from the back seat.

A young Chinook girl, "Probably his granddaughter," George figured aloud, stood upon the porch with her hands clasped before her and said, "Grandfather is expecting you." George whispered to Jake, "The Indians always know when you're coming," and the foreman smiled. The girl took them into a very tidy living room that smelled of smoked salmon and tobacco. Twenty more feet brought them to a solarium in the back. There, they saw a very old man sitting in a chair. The girl stood behind her grandfather and the chief said, "*Kloshe konaway,*" greeting his visitors with a smile and an open hand that beckoned them to sit with him. "I'm Doctor George Madison and this is Jake Larson," George announced. "I telephoned yesterday." Chief Thunder Cloud began to remove his sweater with the help of the girl. Next, he started to roll up his sleeve, until he realized that George didn't have a bag and wasn't prepared to measure the old man's blood pressure. George grinned and confessed, "I'm not that kind of doctor, chief. I'm the county coroner, which is a kind of medical examiner. I mostly deal with folks after they've died." Amused and a little embarrassed, the girl's grandfather readjusted his clothes, smiled, and stated, "Well, if you're not here to help me, then I must be here to help you."

CHAPTER 7

The chief spoke in a clear tone and sounded younger than he looked. His words were unhurried, however, and betrayed his patience and wisdom, along with the prominence he held in the tribe. George leaned forward, resting his forearms upon his knees, and rubbed his hands together as he confessed, "We want to talk to you about the recent drownings along the river." The coroner hesitated a moment, looked briefly at the foreman, then continued, "Also, I guess I want to know if your people have encountered anything," George measured his words carefully, "unusual…and maybe threatening…on, or near, the river." Chief Thunder Cloud smiled. "You mean like the white beavers that want to stop the flow of the Great River?" George frowned, then answered, "No, we were thinking more about monsters…and mermaids." The chief's obstinate tone changed and he spoke to his granddaughter in their native tongue. A moment later, she left the room and his attention returned to his guests. "Would you like to hear a story?"

"Laly ahnkuttie..." the chief began his tale, "Once upon a time, Old Man South Wind was hungry and wandered the land looking for food. He traveled north and came upon an ogress collecting wood from the forest. 'I am hungry,' he told her. 'Can you help me?' The giant, ugly old woman frowned and confessed, 'I have no food.' Then she thought a moment and reached her arm into a great bag that was tied to the belt around her tunic. 'Here!' she exclaimed and pulled out a net, handing it to Old Man South Wind. 'You can use this to catch your dinner.' He thanked her and headed down to the water nearby. Wading out to set his net, it didn't take the old man long to catch a great salmon. Bringing it ashore, he could hear the ogress calling to him from the trees. 'Take heed,' she warned, 'not to cut it crosswise. Instead, you must slit it down its back and split it open.' Old Man South Wind ignored the old woman, waving her away with his knife. Hungrily, he cut into the salmon from top to bottom. The

old man stopped in surprise and stared at the fish as a frightful light stretched out from the hastily made gashes. Bursting forth from the largest wound came an eagle. An eagle so great that his soaring wings blocked out the sun and shook the earth when they flapped. It's eyes flashed with lightning that shimmered and branched out across its body. It was *Sagalie Chak-Chak*...the Thunderbird."

"The Great Bird gathered fir and pine trees from the forest, making a huge nest atop the nearest mountain. There, it laid five great eggs, each a different color." The chief paused a moment when he saw his granddaughter standing in the doorway, just outside of the solarium, holding a pot of tea and three mismatched cups on a tray. Chief Thunder Cloud continued his narrative, filling his pipe with cheap tobacco, as the girl poured the tea and handed a steaming cup to each of the men in the room. "Now, the ogress watched the Thunderbird and saw where it built the nest. She waited until the eagle left the mountain and flew out to sea looking for whales to hunt with its great talons and greater strength." The chief paused, sipping at his tea. "The ogress approached the big, colorful eggs and picked up the nearest one, lifting it out of the nest of trees. She broke its thick shell upon a nearby rock, then she frowned and tossed the broken egg down the mountain. Tumbling down the hill, the egg became a Chinook man, landing on his feet at the base of the slope, before running into the safety of the forest."

Setting a lit match to his pipe, Chief Thunder Cloud smoked from it and said, "The giant, ugly old woman searched on through the nest, taking each egg out and breaking it in disappointment, flinging the broken shell down below. The broken eggs, each a different color, rolled and tumbled down the mountain, each one changing into a young Chinook man of the same color, running toward the trees. The five young men watched as the Thunderbird returned with a freshly caught whale. Discovering what the ogress had done, the great bird set down its dinner and set its vengeful wrath upon the giant old woman, consuming her and the trees of the nest in a wild fire of lightning and flame." Doctor George Madison sat listening, riveted to his seat, as he sipped from his hot cup of tea. Jake left his mug untouched, probably wishing that he had a cup of coffee, George thought.

The chief's voice recaptured the coroner's attention. "The young Chinook men hid in the forest, waiting until sunset before they snuck away. Later that morning, they saw Old Man South Wind using his net to fish for his breakfast. Very hungry, the brave young men approached the old man and asked if he had any food for them. 'Let me teach you to fish,' the old man said and showed them how to use the net given to him by the giantess. Catching several salmon, Old Man South Wind used his knife to slit the fish along their backs. 'Don't just cut them any old way,' he warned the young men. 'Why,' one of them asked, 'what will happen?' Before the old man could answer, the last, uncut fish began to speak. It said, 'If you don't honor our form and admire our beauty, preparing us to eat in a manner that suits us, then we will stop swimming up this river to spawn.' So, the young men each promised the fish, Old Man South Wind, and themselves, that they would always respectfully clean and carve their catch of salmon."

"With their bellies full," the chief went on, "the young men thanked Old Man South Wind and began to journey eastward along the path of the river. They came to a rock and within it they found a woman struggling to grow and break free from her womb. The men helped her out and one of them took her for his wife. As they walked, they discovered three more women and the men helped them to finish their growth and free themselves from the rocks, trees, and flowering plants along the river. Now, four of the young men were married, but the fifth searched in vain for his mate as the tribe traveled east." The foreman set down his mug and looked over at George as if to say, "Where is all of this going?" George caught his glance, but was too engrossed in the story to interrupt the chief. Outside, the light dimmed and heavy drops of rain began to fall as another storm cell slowly rolled beneath the weight of its load and the pushing winds.

Chief Thunder Cloud loaded another pipe full of tobacco and continued, "This last young man, born from the broken egg of the Thunderbird like his brothers, was very lonely. After the tribe had settled, he would wander the land for hours and call out to the woman that he knew was waiting for him to pull her up from the earth. Sitting next to the river one morning, he heard a voice crying above the sound of the rushing water. Looking out through the crisp light of the new day, he saw a woman thrashing about, reaching her arms up through the waves. The young man swam toward her, but she was too far out in the rushing water of the great river and he couldn't reach her. He asked his brothers to help, but none of them could get to her. They spent the rest of the day and the next building a canoe. Three of the men paddled out to where the woman was seen, but she was gone. The lonely young man wept in sadness. He wandered to the spot next to the river and sat every morning, looking for the woman he thought lost beneath the waves."

Sitting forward in his chair, the chief said, "On the fifth day, the young man went to the river with hope in his heart. The clouds were thick and rested upon the earth and the water. All was silent, except for the gentle sound of the water lapping against the rocks and sand of the shore. The young man began to weep quietly to himself, but stopped when he heard what sounded like a gentle song. It flew to him like the spirit of a bird flying blind through the grey mist. As if in a trance, the young man waded out into the water. Singing to him in a voice that he couldn't resist was a woman, his woman, and he moved toward her. He could see that she was different, though, and he watched as she dived and swam easily, submerging and reemerging like she was born in the water. She embraced and held him with her arms, wrapping the lower half of her body around him as they moved together. She gathered his seed before releasing him to float back to the safety of the shoreline."

"When his brothers found him later that morning, he had fish scales and slime on his body, lying in the reeds with his eyes closed and a smile upon his face. The young Chinook was half asleep and didn't want to wake from what seemed like a dream. Standing in a cluster, his brothers heard a splash nearby. They stared at a strange woman and she stared back at them. Suddenly, she surged upward and dived back into the water, revealing herself to be a great salmon from the waste down. They called her, '*Pish Klootchman*…the She-fish.' I just call them 'Water Women,' myself," and the chief chuckled to himself. "As the story went, this water woman took the young man's seed with her and used it to give life to the eggs that she had laid, buried in the watery silt at the bottom of a secret canyon. Another moon passed and the eggs hatched, giving birth to the woman's daughters, each of them part woman above and part fish below. Their eggs only give birth to more water women, though, because the original she-fish wasn't pulled from the river and was forced to finish her form and become whole among the fish of the river."

Chief Thunder Cloud emptied his pipe by gently tapping it against the side of the table next to his chair. As if on cue, his granddaughter carried a tray of food into the room and placed it at the center of the gathering. The guests thanked the girl and each took a sampling of dried salmon and venison. Chewing on a piece of meat, the chief said, "Many years ago, it was still considered an honor among my people to be selected by a she-fish for the sacred joining. Every spring, the strongest young men in the village went down to the large pool at the foot of Multnomah Falls. For three days, they danced, jumped, ran, and wrestled with one another. They chanted and used river rocks to beat the sacred rhythm of the world. Naked, their bodies were painted and the young men took turns standing upon a great flat rock near the water with their arms spread like the waking eagle. They used the warmth and light of the sun to stimulate themselves and demonstrated their size and potency for the she-fish to see."

"After the ceremony, the water women gathered together and rose up from the pool to choose the tallest, strongest, and most handsome of the men. Then, one of the she-fish made motion for the man to enter the water and follow her to where it shallowed. Left alone, the two lovers joined together and their song floated among the branches of the trees throughout the night. Afterward, she released him and he returned to the village the following morning, dazed, and was allowed to rest and recover his strength. Sometimes, the young man slept for a week." Listening, the foreman saw a twinkle in Thunder Cloud's eye before the chief smiled and said, "I know this to be true because I was one of the lucky ones. Every year, the courtship ritual was honored by my people and performed by the young men of the village. It was this way until the white man came. Your ancestors murdered many of our bravest men. When the water women saw the cruelty and ugliness of the white man, they stopped coming to the sacred pool."

Jake choked down his anger in response to the indictment of Western Progress and spoke up. "Listen, chief, where can I find these fish girls?" he abruptly asked. "I think they may have killed two of my workers. Plus, I'd like to know where to send the bill for all the damage those monsters have done to the dam site." The old chief looked sternly at the foreman and said plainly, "Young man, you must understand that the wall you build in the river will change the shape of the land and this change threatens the world of the she-fish. They are attacking you, because you are attacking them." Jake wiped his hands down across his face in exasperation and exclaimed, "Attacking them? How can our project be threatening something that may not even exist?" Chief Thunder Cloud sighed away his patience and said, "The water women are as real as you and me, dam builder. They live and swim and sing in a sacred canyon near the lake at Rooster Rock. It is known among my people as the Canyon of the She-Fish."

The coroner nodded his head and then interrupted by stating, "I know the canyon, but it's inaccessible and off limits to anyone outside of your tribe. It's not like we can just venture over there and take pictures to back up the rest of our evidence." George set down his half-finished cup of tea and said, "I've always known the place as Fish People's Canyon, because of the nearby Indian village and their reliance on fishing." Chief Thunder Cloud nodded in agreement and validated the coroner's point. "Years ago," the chief explained, "my people brought down great rocks and dirt from higher up and blocked the only entrance to the canyon." The foreman interrupted by asking, "How can I get in there? I need to talk with these fish girls and take them to task for what they've done." The old chief chuckled in response to Jake's naive desperation. "Young man," he told the foreman, "you need to be chosen by the water women and taken to the sacred place of joining under their guidance. There is no other way."

Chief Thunder Cloud stood up and faced Jake, recognizing the young man's bravery and good nature. "Paddle out on to the lake that rests in front of the canyon and wait for them. Go early in the morning when the world is quiet and still. If you please them, then one of the water women will show herself to you. After only a glance, you will belong to her, because you will not be able to resist. The she-fish only mate with the strongest, most gifted, and most handsome of young men. They want only the best seed for their eggs, so that these eggs will hatch and give birth to beautiful water girls." Glancing over at a promotional wall calendar from a Portland car dealership, the chief said, "If you choose to show yourself to them, then you must do it very soon. The season of the sacred joining is nearly finished."

Before leaving, George and Jake generously thanked the old chief and his family for their hospitality and time. On the way back toward the dam site, they drove past the small lake that sits along Interstate 84 at Rooster Rock. Excited, Jake said, "I can see the top of the canyon. The entrance is blocked off on the far side of the lake. It looks like the only way I can get there is by boat." Driving, George glanced over and said, "You're right, but are you sure this is a good idea? If these creatures actually exist, they could be more for any one man to handle. You may end up like Old Man Jack. Why don't you let me phone the sheriff and arrange a proper search of the area? After all, we may need a permit. Trespassing is still a crime." The foreman looked over at George and said, "Don't worry. I have an ace up my sleeve." The coroner raised an eyebrow and asked, "Do you feel like sharing?" but Jake slowly shook his head and tried to flatten his smile as he gently sucked the secret back through his teeth.

CHAPTER 8

Jake was already awake at four in the morning when the bells chattered on his alarm clock. He laid there thinking of all of the things that he would rather do on his day off from work. "I didn't agree to this when I took the job," he told himself. "I'll never get paid for all the extra time that I've spent running around after mermaids." He wondered how his time sheet might appear if he did list the additional hours. "Who would believe such a crazy story?" he asked himself in the mirror as he shaved. The foreman had already made arrangements to have a small boat left near the lake and It there when he arrived. The still-dark morning was a cool and damp. A tule fog caressed the surface of the water, creating an eerie scene hinting at unseen mysteries. He maneuvered the boat out toward the center of the lake, but he wasn't sure where to go, or what to do, after that. Patiently fighting the chill in the air, Jake sat in silence for what felt to him like a church service. He knew that the first light of day was close, but the fog and the cold felt much closer.

As he sat in the borrowed boat, Jake's thoughts were lost in the world described by Chief Thunder Cloud. He daydreamed about the young Indian men and how they presented themselves to the fish girls. He wished that he could have been there to see them. Bracing himself on his knees, the foreman took off his shirt and exposed his muscular upper body. He was very proud of his physique, because he worked very hard to keep in shape. "If my body is a temple," he still tells himself, "then it will be fit for the finest of gods." Jake decided to stop undressing at the waste, however, "Or, I'll catch my death of cold," he whispered aloud as a warning to himself. Suddenly, he heard pronounced splash off to the right of the boat.

He turned and looked, but the foreman couldn't see anything definite in the fog. Then, Jake heard something swimming toward him. As the sound drew closer, he saw the head of a woman with long green hair. She stopped moving when she saw that he was looking back at her. In a magically toned voice, she said, "Greetings, young man." Surprised that she spoke his language, Jake turned an anxious smile and responded, "Good morning." The girl slowly swam closer and rose up out of the water, exposing her shapely breast and supple belly. She was the most beautiful creature that Jake had ever seen. It was easy to understand why men were so helpless to resist such intoxicating features.

The creature interrupted the foreman's enchantment by asking, "Wouldn't you like to join me in the water?" Cautiously, Jake stood up in the boat and said very simply, "No, thank you." A sexy frown formed on the face of the woman and she coyly asked, "Why not? I like your appearance very much. Don't you like me?" The foreman hesitated a moment and then answered, "Yes, of course I like you, but not in the way that you wish." She looked at him with a slightly furrowed brow and said, "How can this be? No man has ever denied me before." Again, she asked, "How can this be?" and began to appear flustered to the foreman. Kneeling back down in the boat, Jake shrugged his shoulders slightly and smiled. Uncertain of herself, the fish-girl let herself slide back into the water. "No, please don't go," Jake pleaded. "I need to talk to you," he declared, throwing his voice toward the fish-girl as she swam slowly away. Then, he yelled, "I work at the dam," and she stopped.

Turning around, the creature swam back to the boat in a serpentine motion. Looking up at the foreman, she screamed her challenge in an exotic tone, "Why are you doing this to us?" Taken aback, Jake apologized, "I'm sorry. We only learned about you a short time ago." Taking a breath, the foreman collected himself and explained, "We had no idea that you were anything more than the fanciful product of drunken dreams dreamt by lonely sailors." Kneeling down, he continued, "We need you and your sisters to stop attacking our men and their work. May I talk to your leader, or your queen?" Jake rolled his eyes to himself, wondering if he'd wandered into one of the many pulp fantasy and science-fiction magazines of his youth. He wondered aloud, "Do you even have a leader?"

With calm assurance, the fish-girl answered Jake with a voice that shimmered, "Yes. She is known as 'The Light of the Moon.' Come with me. My name is Morning Star."

Gracefully, she turned and slowly swam in the direction of the canyon, beckoning Jake to follow her in his boat. The foreman was relieved to row out his nervousness as he cut through the water in a series of uneven lurches. The lake shallowed quickly as they approached the far side. The foreman stopped rowing and tossed his legs over the side, taking a shock at the stinging cold of the water. He waded and fought his growing shivers, following several yards behind her with worried thoughts. He knew that there was every chance that he might not make it back alive.

As the two figures approached the overgrown rockslide that blocked the entrance to the canyon, Jake could feel a warmth cutting through the chilly water. Stopping to listen for a moment, he noticed a small stream trickling from the canyon to his left. The foreman wondered if there was a natural hot spring somewhere on the other side. "How nice," he thought to himself, imagining a twilight scene of mermaids lounging upon flat rocks, combing the reeds from each other's hair, and waiting for the moon to rise above the trees. When they reached the landslide that blocked the entrance, he noticed a particularly large rock the size of a school bus. The huge stone was in front of a

small, natural archway that lead into the canyon. Morning Star motioned for Jake to follow her, so he continued
wading through the waste-deep stream water toward the
warmth of the pool in front of him.

When they reached the rock, Jake stopped a moment,
uncertain of where they were headed. Through the dim
morning light, he could see that the big stone was sitting
on what looked like a large rock ledge. The boulder rested
on the ledge with one end down in the water, while the
top jutted into the air at a curious angle. The foreman
watched as Morning Star swam over and inserted her arm
into a space under the big stone. Her hand emerged holding a river rock that was roughly the size of a freshly baked
loaf of bread. Jake looked as she cradled the rock in one
arm and swam slowly along the ledge to the other end of
the big stone. Wading closer, he saw her place the rock re-
trieved from the hole into an impression in the ledge outcropping. To the foreman's astonishment, the large boulder was so perfecting balanced along its deceptive resting
place, that it gently tipped up several feet, providing just
enough head room above the water for the two of them to
enter the canyon together.

On the other side, she motioned him to move back. Wading out of the way, the foreman watched the fish-girl approach the rock face along the great stone. Carved into the side were two holes, one larger and deeper than the other. Morning Star reached up from the water, gripped the bottom of the first hole, and gently pulled the big stone back down. Holding it in place, she took another elongated river rock, warn smooth by the waters of time, and slid it into the larger hole. The fish-girl pushed away from the great, motionless stone, leaving the foreman standing in admiration of the simple genius of the doorway. His bachelor's degree in engineering helped him appreciate the beautifully balanced design of the entrance. Viewed from the lake, the similarity of the rubble made the whole of the landslide appear uniformly impassable, keeping the canyon safe and isolated from the encroaching pioneers and settlers. Turning to follow Morning Star, Jake felt a surge of admiration and respect toward the intelligence and imagination behind such exquisite workmanship. He would never see an Indian, or a Mermaid, the same way again.

CHAPTER 9

The foreman was understandably anxious as he accompanied Morning Star into the canyon. His nerves didn't fair any better when the gentle silence surrounding them was shattered by the shrill screams of the She-Fish. Two fish-girls near the front by the archway saw him first and alerted their sisters with shrieks and yells. Jake shivered and rubbed at his goose-pimpled arms in response to the cacophony. Looking ahead, he quickly dropped into a crouch when a particularly robust fish-girl picked up a large rock with both hands and lifted it above her head as if to hurl it at him. Suddenly, Morning Star shouted a command and the frightening chaos and piercing clamor froze into a scene of quiet attentiveness and reluctant calm.

Using her hands to guide her words, Morning Star spoke to the fish-girls in a language that Jake neither recognized, nor understood. With the peace restored, the gathered group moved deeper into the canyon and the foreman breathed his sighs of relief. After a short hike wading and walking along the stream, he found himself dwarfed as he stood in the center of a long, open area cutting back several hundred yards. Jake slowed his pace, feeling privileged and humble in the presence of such divine, natural beauty. He was genuinely honored to be an outsider allowed into what seemed like a great cathedral, hidden from the modern world in a secret slit in the earth. The foreman's eyes lifted their gaze up along the steep canyon walls to the trees that rested atop, hundreds of feet above. Their branches reached across the opening, almost touching one another as the yellow light of the early morning filtered through them, filling the canyon with a painterly glow common to the brush of Bierstadt. He could hear the morning birds above and listened to the deep, slow-moving stream that ran and gathered along the left side of the canyon wall. Further up and beside the placid pools of water was a long flat area where three more fish-girls sat watching the approaching party.

Morning Star motioned Jake to climb up on to the flat rocks and walk ahead. After some effort to reach the top, the foreman found his best view yet of what appeared to be a box canyon. Again, he was struck by the idyllic beauty and simple warmth of the place. Walking forward, he stepped around pungent piles of raw, half-eaten salmon and trout. He could hear the steady rush of a waterfall and, passing a big rock that served to shield the sound and view beyond, he saw a large group of three dozen fish-girls. They kept their distance by hiding in the alcoves along the wall, or remaining mostly submerged beneath the water. Jake could see that there were women of all ages, some even nursing young fish-girls as the mothers sheltered beneath a protective outcropping of rock on the far side of the canyon. The spectacular waterfall danced and sprayed nearby, its high waters steadily replenishing the stream-fed pools along the bottom.

On the right side of the canyon, Jake balanced his steps along a narrow path in the rock as he followed Morning Star. She glided through the pool beside him, swimming just ahead as they approached the roar of the falls. Coming up alongside the waterfall, Jake could see the entrance to a tunnel in the recessed rock behind the cascade. Flowing up and out of the hole beneath a steam that mixed with the mist of the falls was steady flow of hot water. "This must be the source of the hot spring," he quietly declared to himself. Distracted by the deafening din of the water-fall, Jake almost stepped on Morning Star's outstretched fist. She opened it, handing the foreman two small, white pearls, each with a hole drilled through it. She motioned for him to put them into his ears. After a moment, he finished doing as she asked, adjusting them so that the hole in each pearl faced both inward and outward. To the foreman's amazement, the devices worked wonderfully in shutting out the majority of the noise from the falling water, but filtering through the other surrounding sounds. "We could sure use these at the dam site," he thought.

Morning Star motioned for Jake to wait where he stood and then she slowly emerged from the water, pulling and pushing herself up on to the ledge. Amazed, the foreman watched as she made her way across the wet rock floor by sliding and slithering with her lower body, using her arms to both balance and drag herself along. In the available light, Jake noticed the sparkling layers of tiny silver fish scales upon Morning Star's back. Jake thought to himself that these must be the fish scales the coroner was finding under the fingernails of the drowned fishermen. As he watched her move away from him, he could see that the scales were several times larger from her waste down. For a moment, he was transfixed with the flickering light that reflected from the greenish blue hues of her powerful looking tail. He could see why she was such an accomplished swimmer. After a dozen yards, he saw the fish-girl approach the figure of another of her kind laying upon a bed of water grass. This girl was no girl, however, and Jake began to notice her age and the lack of color in her hair. She was an old fish-woman.

Feeling tired, but also antsy and impatient, the foreman fought his eagerness to speak with the matriarch. He sat down to rest his legs and quietly waited to confront the old woman. He rested his eyes and listened to the rhythmic rush of the waterfall. After a moment, Jake noticed an odd smell in the air. It didn't stink, but the sharpness of the odor cut through the wet freshness of the cavern. The foreman decided that the air smelled more like the ocean, rather than the river. Relaxed, he opened his eyes and began to examine the cave in the available light. He noticed piles of shells that had likely belonged to freshwater clams and mussels. There was a reed serving platter nearby and on it were several varieties of water plants, along with two medium-sized crayfish.

Looking past the plate of food, something else caught his wandering eyes. There were small, broken pieces of colored glass strewn about the floor of the cavern. He could see the sleeping hues of blue, green, and red randomly patterned and partially buried in the silted crevasses in the rock shelf. Enchanted, Jake watched their magical reflections occasionally appear and softly shimmer as the light found them hiding among the stones of the cave floor. Closer to where the old woman lay, Jake saw what looked to be several neatly stacked piles of golden rocks on a stone dais. At the bottom of the stacks were nuggets the size of golf balls. Something glimmered along the wall near the rock table and distracted Jake from the treasure displayed upon it. Attached to numerous hanging reeds and dried vines were what looked to be many dozen fish hooks and brightly colored lures. Looking over at the oddly shaped blanket that covered the old woman, Jake peered closer and fought both shock and anger when he realized that it was a collection of drab fishing vests patterned among many brightly colored life jackets. In reluctant silence, Jake quietly hoped that these out-of-place objects didn't represent the spoils of their hidden war with the dam builders of the world.

Interrupting the foreman's visual examination of the cave, Morning Star motioned Jake with her arms to come and sit beside the old woman. Walking slowly over to her place of rest, he could see that she was very old. The woman had very long silvery hair that had a lifetime's worth of polished beads and cleaned shells woven into the stranded weight. To Jake's pleasant surprise, the matriarch still appeared beautiful as she displayed her opalescent tail along with her still firmly pronounced breasts. The old woman looked up at Jake and used a voice distilled by the ages to say, "Star tells me you do not have lust for women. How is this so?" Jake just smiled and confidently changed the subject by saying, "Ma'am, we need to talk about the problems at the new dam site. Your girls have to stop the vandalism. My people have put traps out to catch them," he lied. "They've also placed explosive charges in the river. It's no longer safe for your people to venture near the dam."

Pleadingly, the woman cried out, "Look around, land-walker. If you finish building the great wall in the water, you will flood our home. We know it is true to say that white men stand triumphant upon a conquered world, leaving beings such as us with fewer places to live. Even though we tried remaining hidden from you and your ways, your constant need to change the land is changing us, as well. Now, you force us not just to hide, but to flee and escape into a world that holds little in the way of refuge for our kind. Whatever are we to do?" the old woman asked out of breath and began to weep, turning her face away from the ghostly looking stranger standing before her. Morning Star placed a webbed hand upon the foreman's shoulder and guided him back away from the grieving woman. Confused, Jake moved along with the fish-girl, but then was struck by a displaced memory.

On his very first day on the job at the dam site, he was in his boss's office when another man entered and urgently placed a thick manila folder on the far corner of the desk.

His boss, Don Coleman, seemed to turn pale after glancing at the first page of the report. He asked Jake to please go, have a cup of coffee, and come back later. Jake new something was up, so he waited just outside the closed door for a few minutes and listened. Although much of the conversation was muffled and muted, the foreman did manage to make out the voice of his boss who said, "Why didn't you show me this weeks ago?" The other man, a geologist on the project, responded by explaining, "I just got the report today, sir." Finally, Jake thought that he heard his boss say, "We have to keep this quiet."

Mustering the last of his day's allotment of courage, the foreman stopped and looked back at the old woman sitting upon her bed. In a voice displaying confidence and hope, he announced, "We have one year before the scheduled completion of the dam. Let me see what I can do to help. Please, don't relocate prematurely and, most importantly, stop your girls from damaging the work site and attacking my men. Right now, I need you to help me to help you." The old woman sat in silence for a moment before giving Jake a slow nod of agreement. Then, she thanked him for showing the conviction and courage to come into their secret canyon. Feeling as though he was due some overtime pay for his efforts, Jake lightheartedly followed Morning Star out of the canyon and back to the boat. Outside of the canyon, he wondered what he would do with the rest of his Sunday. Sitting in the boat, the foreman held up a hand as he watched the fish-girl return to her sisterhood, then he began to paddle back to the far shore. The fog was gone and the early morning sunlight bathed the lake with the promise of safety and better days ahead.

CHAPTER 10

That afternoon, Jake only expected to encounter the security detail at the dam site. Checking in, he was relieved to find that he was correct in his assumption. Parking in the usual spot, he meandered over to his boss's trailer thirty yards away. Without a key, he figured that he'd give the lock a jimmy and had a tool ready for the job. "The guards should figure that it's just another incident of vandalism," he thought to himself. Normally averse to criminal activity, Jake felt the subversive enjoyment and darkly euphoric thrill that naughty behavior provides. "These old trailers are so easy to get into," he quietly declared to himself after the door popped open with a brief creak. Countering the sting of his guilty conscience, the foreman continued talking to himself in a low voice. It helped to distract him from his unusual behavior, while focusing his attention on the task at hand.

"Now, where do I look for those papers?" the foreman asked himself. "If I needed to hide them here, where would I stash them?" Jake breathed in and around his outspoken questions as he padded his steps and paced about the trailer. "I would put them at the back of a bottom drawer, beneath everything else, where no one would see them but me!" the foreman stated plainly like an eight-year old figuring out where his parents are hiding the Christmas presents. Sure enough, the documents were right where he thought they should be. Jake sat down at the moderately sized, unadorned desk and opened the file. Reading a moment, he identified the threat almost immediately.

On the second page, there was a topographical map with a red line starting at the base of Mt. hood. Jake followed it with his finger. The line ran to the northwest, across the Columbia River, and stopped at the location of the dam site. Reading the report, he scanned a time line that showed the contents and position of the land over the last ten thousand years. There were clear signs of at least one large earthquake since the last ice age. "How can they do this?" Jake asked aloud. "That's an active fault line! Sure, they've already spent millions of dollars on the current site, but they can't build it there! A quake could strike at any time." Fighting fatigue and the worst kind of surprise, the foreman made mimeograph copies of several pages in the report and then placed the folder back in the drawer.

Although he was exhausted from a full day's worth of adventure, Jake had trouble sleeping through the night. He knew that when he arrived at work the next morning, he stood a poor chance of avoiding his boss. He listened to the faucet slowly drip into the bathroom sink and watched the play of stray car beams cut through his partially curtained window and glide across the ceiling above his bed. Should he say something about what he knew? If so, then what exactly? After much sleepless deliberation, the foreman decided that If he said anything directly, that he would be fired for some reason, or another, and he needed the job. "I think I'll go talk to Sheriff Wilson," he muttered to himself in relief and finally fell back to sleep.

From the dam site later that morning, Jake placed a call to the Clark County Sheriff. "You should be able to catch me in the office after twelve," Larry told the foreman. "If you miss me there, then you can usually find me down at the diner after mid-day." Jake thanked him and said, "I'll be there." Always prompt, he arrived at the Sheriff's Department right on time. He knew that he was taking a chance, but he felt that he could trust him. Plus, he wasn't sure what else to do. After a cursory knock at the frame of the open door to Sheriff Parker's office, the foreman walked in and set down a large brown envelope on the only uncluttered part of the desk that stood near the window. "Thanks again for seeing me, Sheriff. Please pardon the cloak-and-dagger routine, but I need to leave this with you. You probably know someone over at the New Columbia Gazette who will find this story more than just interesting reading. I can't stay and, if anyone asks, I was never here. Thanks again, Sheriff," and with that, the foreman shuffled out of the office as quickly as he entered.

* * *

As the days turned into weeks, there were no more incidents of vandalism, nor were there any mysterious drownings to investigate. Every morning, Jake stopped by his local grocer on the way to work and bought a newspaper, looking for stories on the dam site. Day after day, the paper contained nothing more than the sort of peaceful, undramatic news that one can expect living in a relatively quiet place. After another weekend of worry and woe, the foreman decided to let things be and to get back to his normal routine. "If you can't beat 'em," he caught himself saying aloud as he drove past the grocer without stopping and headed straight to work. Driving up the gravel path, he was surprised to see a cluster of people and activity near the front gate of the dam site. "Monday mornings are busy around here," he said to himself beneath a furrowed brow, "but not like this."

Idling the engine, Jake rolled down his driver-side window. "What's going on?" he asked one of the security guards who was standing away from the hullabaloo. "There's some big hubbub in the Gazette," the guard responded. Excited, Jake managed a shaky three-point turn in his truck and drove to the nearest coffee shop. His hands began to shake from the anxiety of the moment. He steadied one of them and fished through the loose change at the bottom of his pocket. Finding the proper coin, he was almost afraid to read the paper after he had it in his grasp. If Sheriff Wilson gave him up, then his career was over. It was that simple. Or, he would have to tell his boss about the fish people to save his job. That move would probably send him off to the loony bin. "I'm between a Rooster Rock and a hard place," he joked to himself.

Jake was instantly relieved when he read that the source of the story was, and would remain, anonymous. The rest of the piece detailed the history of the landscape around the dam site and, as newspaper writing can do, portrayed a grim picture of what a good-sized earthquake would do to the dam and the region around it. Exhaling a deep sigh through his growing smile, Jake was very pleased with himself as he drove back to the job site. He walked so fast that he practically ran into his boss's trailer, saying, "What do we do now?" In a surprisingly calm and assured voice, Don Coleman responded, "We move to plan B." Jake sat down in a chair across from Don's desk. "Plan B?" he asked. "Yep," his boss answered, "and 'B' stands for 'Bonneville.'"

CHAPTER 11

The following Sunday, Jake returned to the canyon of the fish-girls. This time, they were not afraid of him. Morning Star greeted the foreman with a wave of her webbed hand and asked, "What brings you here, dam-builder?" Jake smiled and said, "I have good news. We're moving the dam upriver and its new location will not threaten your home." Beaming with joy, Morning Star asked, "Please, come and tell Grandmother Moon the good news." After the trek into the canyon and up to the grotto behind the waterfall, Jake followed behind Morning Star and they approached the old woman. Right away, he sensed that she was near the end of her days. Leaning up on her elbows, the old matriarch appeared almost transparent in the flickering light within the cave. It looked as though she was slowly fading away. Jake shared his news and it made her eyes smile as she listened. "Thank you, land-walker," she said, taking the foreman's hand and holding it for a moment.

"I come bearing gifts," Jake announced and reached into the small satchel resting at his side. From it, he removed a gold chain fastened to a crystal pendulum in the shape of a teardrop. "I brought this for you," he said, "and I should have enough here to give one to each of your girls." He held it up to the sunlight near the entrance of the cave and let it slowly twist and twirl. Gently spinning, the prism split the white light into a parade of little rainbows. The colors danced and shimmered, jumping about the walls of the grotto. The foreman took a step outside and let the pendulum catch a clear beam of sunlight. In a lovely and unexpected display, the twisting prism showered the shaded canyon with a circus of color. The magical, moving manifestation of hue and light caught the attention of several fish girls nearby and they began to sing almost spontaneously. Soon, all of the girls were gathered together, singing and bathing and grooming one another as they enjoyed the pretty play of light.

Stepping backward into the grotto, the foreman allowed the pendulum to slow and end the show. Finally, he turned and walked back to where the old woman lay and put the necklace into her hand. "Now," Jake said in a voice made of sterner stuff, "there is something that you can do for me and my people. Your girls need to stop drowning the young men with whom they choose to mate." With furrowed brow, the old woman frowned. "If we let them live," she explained, "then they will tell their tales. Soon after, everyone would know about us. Eventually, your women and your priests would hunt us down as a threat. Next, your fishermen would scoop us from the water and stuff us as trophies mounted beneath their pride. Those of us who remain would be captured, studied, and displayed by your scientists and your showmen." The old woman winced at a touch of pain brought on by the burden and focus of her rant. Catching her breath, she finished by saying, "If we let the white seed-bearers live, then you might as well build your dam right on top of us, because we cannot survive your ways."

Sitting down beside the old woman, Jake said, "I understand and sympathize with your concerns. In fact, you are probably right about all of your fears coming to pass as things stand. But, I have a plan." Sharing an encouraging look with the old woman, the foreman explained, "You see, my mother was a gypsy and she taught me many things before she died. From the wealth of her knowledge and wisdom, what I want to share with you and your people is the power of hypnotism." The old woman's eyes drifted away from her visitor as she sighed, "We already use the power of enchantment. What can you teach us about a gift that we already possess?" Jake nodded and said, "Well, I suspect that the two techniques are as similar as they are different. I will teach your girls how to use the pendulum to make men forget. It can also be used to help them remember. My mother taught me the way to lock and unlock the minds of men. Now, I want to teach you and your girls the same skill. You can still use your magical ways to charm men and bring them to your embrace, but then you can use hypnotism to send them safely back into their world and the waiting arms of their wives and girlfriends."

Grandmother Moon looked over at Morning Star and asked, "Is this possible, child?" The foreman interrupted the girl's quizzical shoulder shrug by saying, "Yes, it is more than possible. I can teach you all, just as I was taught." The old woman finally smiled and seemed relieved. Her peaceful presence was infectious and Jake felt a gentle, but very powerful surge of positive emotion that brought his eyes to water with the tears of success. Seeing his reaction, the old woman leaned over to his ear and spent several moment whispering to the foreman. Jake patiently listened as he used a finger to quickly wipe away the oddly fallen tear. Then, she pointed at an arrangement of nuggets, coins, and gemstones in the corner of the cave near her bed.

Jake glanced at the pile of wealth, looked at the old woman, and then turned his attention to Morning Star. The young fish-girl smiled and said, "Yes, please, take as much as you like. It is our gift to you." Suppressing his excitement, the foreman casually filled his pockets with a sampling of the treasure, thinking to himself, "This will sure help to pay me back for all of the time and money that I've spent dealing with this crazy mystery. Nancy Drew, you can eat your heart out." Hugging the old woman, Jake promised to return each Sunday and teach her children the art of hypnotism. Before following Morning Star out of the canyon and back to the boat, he reassured the dying woman with his best attempt at poetry. "The next mating season," he said, "along with each and every one that follows, can be depended upon to come and go with the softly secret touch of a morning fog upon still, peaceful waters."

* * *

As the weeks turned into months, the construction of the new dam at Bonneville moved along at a steady clip. Every Sunday found Jake in the canyon as he promised. The foreman patiently worked with and ultimately finished his guidance and instruction of the fish-girls in learning his technique in the art of hypnosis. Sadly, Grandmother Moon passed away as expected and the next eldest fish-woman took her place in the grotto behind the waterfall. Having finished with his time among the fish-girls of the secret canyon, Jake knew that he had one more thing to do before getting on with the rest of his life and work.

The foreman rang the coroner, who in turn rang the sheriff and three men found several hours to share

amidst their busy schedules. Skipping the bottle of bourbon this time, they drove over to Old Man Jack's place
to share the rest of the story with him. Keeping the canyon's location and entrance a secret, Jake still managed
to entertain the group and boost the old man's spirit
by sharing his experience. This wasn't the only reason
that he wanted to talk with the old man, however, and
the foreman changed his tone before continuing. "You
didn't tell us," he challenged the old man, "that your
girlfriend was pregnant with your son when you were
attacked. The fish-woman, Moon, told me that she was
the one that mated with you. She also wanted me to tell
you that she is deeply sorry for what happened to you."
Listening, Old Man Jack sat in his chair and stared at
the deck beneath his boots. A long moment passed and
the old man finally returned his gaze toward the Sunday
afternoon eyes of his unexpected company.

Finally, he confessed, "I'll be damned for filling up
my life with anger and hatred, drowning it all in booze."
Jake thought that he saw a tear stream down through the
dirt and grime upon the old man's cheek. Posturing with
sympathy and understanding, the coroner said, "It's not

too late to change, old man. The good news is that you don't have to learn any new tricks, but simply relearn old ones that you forgot you knew. Apparently, you not only have a son, but three grandchildren. We have their address and phone number. The Sheriff, here, and I were able to do some leg work based upon what Jake told us after his adventure." Softening his tone even more, George said, "Old Man, it's never too late when you're still in the game. Why don't you look up your kin and reconnect? You might be able to spend what's left of your life with them, watching your grandkids grow up. Anyhow, think about it. We all wanted to come and tell you, so that you knew we were being legitimate."

The old man nodded up and down and thanked his visitors for coming. George said, "I hope that we didn't open your old wounds too wide. We just thought that you might want to know what we discovered and maybe put some things to rest." While the three men quietly spoke with one another, Sheriff Parker noticed Jake pull something from his pants pocket and place it on the table next to the old man's favorite chair. The sheriff redirected his attention toward George as Jake turned and approached the group. "Are you guys ready to go?" the foreman asked and the three men parted ways with the old man and wished him all the best in courage and luck.

Watching them walk back up the pier, Old Man Jack returned to his chair and let out a big sigh. Turning to his left, he blinked and shook his head at the sight before his tired eyes. On the table was a small pile of small, precious gemstones. Amidst the sparkling hues of green, red, and blue rested a yellowish nugget of nearly pure gold. Astonished, the old man ran the fingers of his left hand over the stones and picked the nugget up to hold tightly in his fortunate palm. He pressed his fist firmly against his forehead and whispered to himself. He made a promise to change his ways. Instead of heading over to the bar, or state-licensed liquor store to celebrate with a bottle, Old Man Jack walked to the nearest pay phone and made the important call of his life.

* * *

To this day, on warm spring days that make you think that it's already summer, you can see young men walking naked and in full bloom upon the banks of the Columbia River. They strut about and show their manliness, wrestling and posturing, as they explore the character and geography of Rooster Rock State Park. Appearing in a youthful daze, they don't know why they find themselves there, or why they come back, time and again, season after season.... What they do know is more of a vague sort of feeling, rather than a thought. The hazy sort of pleasant feeling that a person can have after a wonderful dream that has otherwise lost its detail. A good, deeply powerful feeling telling them that wonderful things happen at this park, while reminding them that some mysteries are best kept secret.

A special thanks to Kristin Summers of redbat design in La Grande, Oregon for her outstanding editing of my three books. Thanks to her expertise, *The Hungry Cabin*, *The Plane Full of Protein*, and *The Fish People's Canyon* are available through Amazon.com and book stores across the country.

www.PatrickColeman.weebly.com

Made in the USA
Coppell, TX
12 March 2022